Big Head!

Written by Jane Clarke

Illustrated by Jan Smith

Collins

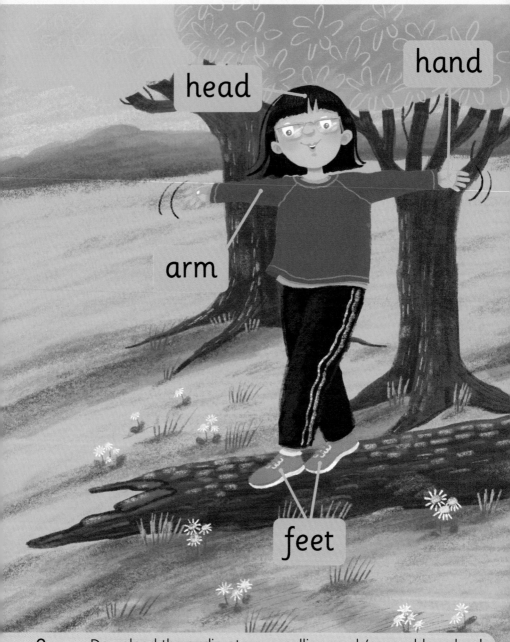

head

hand

arm

feet

leg

foot

This is Eva. Eva runs.

This is Ana. Ana runs.

Look, Ana! Look, Eva!
A leg and a foot.

And an arm. The arm is big!

Look! Two arms. Two legs.
Two feet. One big head!

9

Oh, no! Goodbye, arms.
Goodbye, legs.

Goodbye, Big Head!

Look! Two hands.

1 Look and tell the story

After reading

2 Listen and say

Collins

Published by Collins
An imprint of HarperCollins*Publishers*
Westerhill Road
Bishopbriggs
Glasgow
G64 2QT

HarperCollins*Publishers*
1st Floor, Watermarque Building
Ringsend Road
Dublin 4
Ireland

William Collins' dream of knowledge for all began with the publication of his first book in 1819.

A self-educated mill worker, he not only enriched millions of lives, but also founded a flourishing publishing house. Today, staying true to this spirit, Collins books are packed with inspiration, innovation, and practical expertise. They place you at the center of a world of possibility and give you exactly what you need to explore it.

© HarperCollins*Publishers* Limited 2021

10 9 8 7 6 5 4 3 2 1

ISBN 978-0-00-848796-6

Collins® and COBUILD® are registered trademarks of HarperCollins*Publishers* Limited

www.collins.co.uk/elt

British Library Cataloguing in Publication Data

A catalogue record for this publication is available from the British Library.

Author: Jane Clarke
Illustrator: Jan Smith (Beehive)
Series editor: Rebecca Adlard
Publishing manager: Lisa Todd
Product managers: Jennifer Hall and Caroline Green
In-house editor: Alma Puts Keren
Project manager: Emily Hooton
Editors: Emma Wilkinson and Samantha Lacey
Proofreaders: Natalie Murray and Michael Lamb
Cover designer: Kevin Robbins
Typesetter: 2Hoots Publishing Services Ltd
Audio produced by White House Sound Ltd
Reading guide author: Emma Wilkinson
Production controller: Rachel Weaver
Printed and bound by: Pureprint Group, UK

Download the audio for this book and a reading guide for parents and teachers at www.collins.co.uk/peapoddownloads